Eoin McLaughlin  Polly Dunbar

The Hug

Hedgehog was feeling sad.
As sad as a hedgehog can feel.
So sad only one thing could help.

"Hello," said Hedgehog.

"Hello," said Fox.

"Please may I have a hug?" asked Hedgehog.

"I'd love to," replied Fox, "but I've just got to knock over that bin."

"I'm feeling quite sad and would *very* much like a hug," said Hedgehog.

"I'm a little busy
counting all of
my nuts,"
replied Squirrel,

who only had
three nuts.

"Now I'll have to start over.
One . . . Two . . . Three . . ."

"Might *you* give me just a small hug?"
begged Hedgehog.

"Perhaps after I sing my song,"
replied Magpie, "which is quite long."

Sssqquuaawwwkkk ssssquua

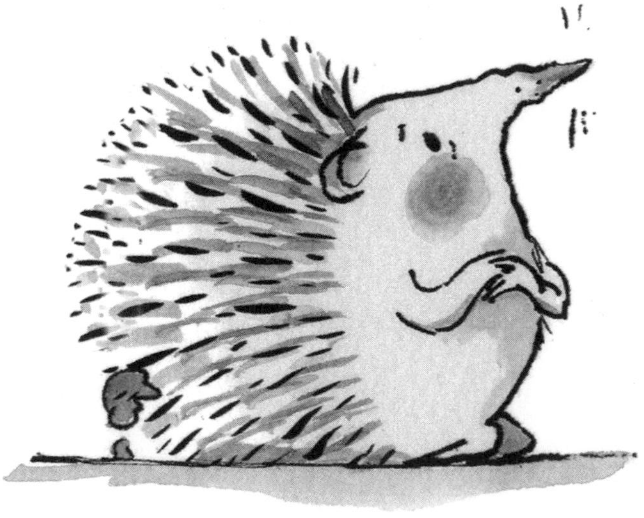

"Why will no one hug me?" Hedgehog sniffed.

"You're just a little bit tricky to hug," replied Owl, "with all your prickly prickles. But don't worry, there's someone for everyone."

"Now I am even more sad," said Hedgehog.
"Will I *ever* find someone to hug?"

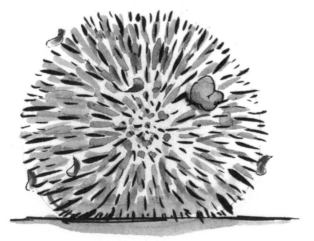

And that's when . . .

they

met.

And . . . that's . . .

when . . . they . . .

hugged . . .

As happy as a hug
can make you . . .

As happy as two
someones can be.

when . . .   they . . .

And . . . that's . . .

met.

they

And that's when . . .

"Now I am even more sad," said Tortoise.
"Will I *ever* find someone to hug?"

"It's your shell," replied Owl.
"It's just so very hard.
But don't worry.
There's someone
for everyone."

"Why will no one hug me?" asked Tortoise.

"Not today," replied Frog. "Sorry,
but I have to jump over there now."

"Do *you* have time for a quick hug?"
asked Tortoise.

"Not right now,"
said Rabbit.
"Unfortunately
I'm digging a very
important hole."

"Might I trouble *you* for a small hug?"
asked Tortoise.

"I'm sorry, but my hands are sticky," replied Badger.

"Might you give me a big hug?" asked Tortoise.

"Hello," said Badger.

"Hello," said Tortoise.

Tortoise was feeling sad.
As sad as a tortoise can feel.
So sad only one thing could help.

Eoin McLaughlin ★ Polly Dunbar

The Hug